CLEVER DUCK

TAKE OFF WITH A KITE!

This lively series is designed for children who have developed reading fluency and enjoy reading complete books on their own.

The stories are attractively presented with plenty of illustrations which make them satisfying and fun! A perfect follow-on from the Read Alone series.

DICK KING-SMITH

CLEVER DUCK

ILLUSTRATED BY MIKE TERRY

VIKING

VIKING

Published by the Penguin Group
Penguin Books Ltd, 27 Wrights Lane, London W8 5TZ, England
Penguin Books USA Inc., 375 Hudson Street, New York, New York 10014, USA
Penguin Books Australia Ltd, Ringwood, Victoria, Australia
Penguin Books Canada Ltd, 10 Alcorn Avenue, Toronto, Ontario, Canada
M4V 3B2
Penguin Books (NZ) Ltd, 182–190 Wairau Road, Auckland 10, New Zealand

Penguin Books Ltd, Registered Offices: Harmondsworth, Middlesex, England

First published 1996
10 9 8 7 6 5 4 3 2 1

Text copyright © Fox Busters Limited, 1996
Illustrations copyright © Mike Terry, 1996

The moral right of the author has been asserted

Filmset in Linotron Palatino 14/22 pt by
Rowland Phototypesetting Limited, Bury St Edmunds, Suffolk
Printed in Great Britain by Butler & Tanner Limited, Frome and London

A CIP catalogue record for this book is available from the British Library

ISBN 0–670–86143–X

Contents

1. "Ignoramus"

"Ignoramuses!" said Mrs Stout. "That's what they are. Ignoramuses, every one of them."

"Who, dear?" asked her friend, Mrs Portly.

"Why, the other animals on this farm, of course."

"Leaving aside us pigs, you mean?" said another friend, Mrs O'Bese.

"Naturally, Mrs O'Bese," replied Mrs Stout. "All pigs are born with a high degree of intelligence, that goes without saying." There came grunts of agreement from the other sows – Mrs Chubby, Mrs Tubby, Mrs Swagbelly and Mrs Roly-Poly – as they rooted in the mud of their paddock.

"I am speaking," went on Mrs Stout, "of such creatures as the cows . . ."

"Dullards!" put in Mrs Chubby.

". . . and the sheep . . ."

"Simpletons!" said Mrs Tubby.

". . . and the chickens . . ."

"Morons!" said Mrs Swagbelly.

". . . and the ducks."

"Idiots!" cried Mrs Roly-Poly. "Imbeciles! Half-wits! Dimwits! Nitwits!"

"Just so," said Mrs Stout. "Each and every other creature on the farm is, as I said, an ignoramus. Why, there's not one of them that would even know what the word meant."

"Surely, dear," said Mrs Portly, "they couldn't be that stupid?"

"There's one sure way to find out," said Mrs O'Bese.

Unlike the others, Mrs O'Bese was an Irish pig, with an Irish sense of humour, and it struck her that here was a chance for a bit of fun.

On one side of the sows' paddock was a field in which the dairy herd was grazing, and Mrs O'Bese made her way up to the fence, close to which one of the cows stood watching her approach.

"Good morning," said Mrs O'Bese.

"Good moo-ning," said the cow.

"Are you," asked Mrs O'Bese, "an ignoramus?"

"Noo," said the cow. "I'm a Friesian."

Mrs O'Bese went to a second side of the paddock, where there was a field full of sheep, and spoke to one.

"Hey, ewe!" she said.

"Me?" said the sheep.

"Yes, you. Who did you think I was talking to?"

"Ma?" said the sheep.

Some mothers do have 'em, thought the sow.

"Ignoramus," she said.

"Baa," said the sheep.

"D'you know what it means?"

14

"Na, na," said the sheep.

"Well," said Mrs O'Bese, "that cow over there is one and you are too."

"Na, na," said the sheep. "Me not two. Me one."

Mrs O'Bese shook her head so that her ears flapped.

"Ass," she grunted.

"Na, na," said the sheep. "Me ewe."

On a third side of the paddock was an orchard with a duckpond in it. A flock of chickens was pecking about under the apple trees, and there was a number of ducks, some walking around, some swimming in the pond.

Mrs O'Bese addressed a hen.

"Ignoramus," she said.

"What?" said the hen.

"Ignoramus. That's what you are, isn't it?"

"I don't get you," said the hen.

"It's a word," said Mrs O'Bese, "used to describe someone who has very little knowledge."

"Knowledge?" said the hen. "What does that mean?"

Mrs O'Bese sighed.

"How many beans make five?" she said.

The hen put her head on one side, consideringly.

"What's a bean?" she said.

"Oh, go and lay an egg!" said Mrs O'Bese.

"OK," said the hen, and went.

A duck waddled past.

I'll try a different approach, thought the Irish sow. Maybe I've been too abrupt. I'll turn on the charm, a bit of the old blarney.

"Top of the mornin' to ye, me fine

friend!" she cried. "Would you be after sparin' me a minute of your valuable time?"

The duck stopped. It was an ordinary sort of bird, brown and white in colour, and looking, Mrs O'Bese thought, as stupid as all its kind. It stared at her with beady eyes.

Then it said, "Quack!"

At this moment Mrs O'Bese heard the sound of heavy bodies squelching through the mud, and looked round to see that Mrs Stout and Mrs Portly, Mrs Chubby, Mrs Tubby, Mrs Swagbelly and Mrs Roly-Poly were all standing behind her.

"Listen to this," she grunted softly at them, and to the duck she said, loudly and slowly as one does to foreigners, "Now then, my friend. I wonder if perhaps you'd be able to help me.

18

There's this long word I've heard and I'm just a silly old sow, so I don't know the meaning of it."

"Quack!" said the duck again.

"The word," said Mrs O'Bese, "is 'ignoramus'."

"Is that so?" said the duck.

"Yes. Can you tell me what it means?"

"I must say," said the duck, "you surprise me. I had been under the distinct impression that pigs were reasonably intelligent. If you don't know what an ignoramus is, then you must be one."

2. Ed-u-cation

The seven sows stood in shocked silence as the duck waddled away.

Then a black-and-white sheepdog came trotting across the orchard and approached the duck, tail wagging.

"Good morning, Damaris," said the dog.

"It was a good morning, Rory," said the duck, "until just now. Those sows! They are *so* patronizing. They think that they're so intelligent and that the rest of us are fools. They need to be taught a lesson."

Rory stared thoughtfully at the sows.

"You're right, Damaris," he said, "I wouldn't mind wiping those smug smiles off their fat faces. I'll think of something."

"I'm sure you will, Rory," said Damaris. "You're miles cleverer than them anyway. I should know. If it hadn't been for you, I'd just be an ordinary duck."

An ordinary duck Damaris certainly was not. That is to say, she was not stupid and thoughtless and empty-headed as most ducks are. On the contrary, she was educated, and her teacher had been Rory. It had happened like this.

All sheepdogs are born with the instinct for herding things, and they

begin as soon as they can run around.
Rory as a puppy had often come into the
orchard, practising his craft upon the
chickens and ducks. The hens squawked
and flapped and ran out of his way, but
the ducks were slower moving and
tended, like sheep, to bunch together,
and, like sheep, to protest loudly at
being forced to go this way and that.

Usually they managed to make their way to the pond, where the puppy could not follow, but one morning he came upon a mother duck with a brood of baby ducklings, and Rory set himself to keep these little ones away from the water.

For some time he moved them here and there, while the duck quacked distractedly in the background, but then a strange thing happened. One of the ducklings flatly refused to move any further. It simply sat down in the grass, seemingly unafraid of what must have appeared to it a very large animal, while the rest hurried off to join their mother.

The puppy sniffed at the duckling.

"What's the matter?" he said.

"The matter," piped the duckling, "is that you're a big bully and I'm tired."

"I was only practising," said Rory.

"What for?"

"Herding sheep. That's what I shall be doing. When I'm grown up. I'm a sheepdog, you see. My name's Rory. What's yours?"

"Damaris," said the duckling.

"That's a nice name," said Rory.

Ducks were silly animals, he knew that, his mother had told him, but this one seemed quite sensible.

"Look, Damaris," he said, "I'm sorry if I've upset you. Like I said, I have to practise – it's all part of my education."

"Ed-u-cation?" said the duckling. "What does that mean?"

"Why, learning things, being taught things you wouldn't otherwise know."

"Who teaches you?" asked Damaris.

"My mum. Doesn't your mum teach you?"

Does she, Damaris thought? She didn't teach me to swim, I did that on my own,

24

and the same with walking or running or
eating or speaking. Yet here was this dog
being taught things, like herding sheep. I
don't suppose I could do that, but, all the
same, it would be nice to have a proper –
what was it? – education. I wonder –
could Rory teach me?

And, indeed, that was how things
turned out.

That first meeting between puppy and duckling led, as time went by, to a regular friendship between dog and duck.

Every day the young Rory would come and spend time with the young Damaris, and pass on to his friend all the things that he had learned. And because dogs – and especially sheepdogs – are highly intelligent creatures, and perhaps because Rory was a particularly bright sheepdog, and certainly because Damaris

was most anxious to learn about the world in a way no duck had ever done before, teacher and pupil worked wonderfully well together.

One day, about a year after their first meeting, the two friends were chatting together out in the orchard. Conversation was something they much enjoyed, something that was denied the other ducks, who only ever spoke to one another in monosyllables.

"Grub up" (when the farmer brought

their food), "Nice day" (when it was pouring with rain), and suchlike brief sentences were the limits of their conversational powers.

"In the matter of intelligence," Damaris said, "to which creature on the farm would you give the highest marks?"

Rory yawned.

"Me," he said.

"Dogs in general, you mean?"

"Yes."

"And the lowest?"

"Your lot, I suppose," said Rory.

"Ah," said Damaris. "So I am one of the stupidest creatures on the farm?"

Rory got to his feet, tail wagging.

"No, Damaris," he said. "You're different. You are a clever duck."

3. A Lovely Little Scheme

Now, in summer-time some months later, as they stood and looked at the seven sows, Rory said, "Why have you got your feathers in a twist anyway? What did they say to you?"

"One of them asked me the meaning of a word," said Damaris. "Pretended she didn't know it. I was watching her before, going round to the cows and to the sheep, and she spoke to a hen too, tried it on all of them, I bet."

"What word?" said Rory.

"'Ignoramus'. As if I didn't know."

"Typical," said Rory. "Trying to make other animals feel small. I've got a good mind to go out there and bite one or two of their fat backsides. Oh, they're so smug!"

"Look!" said Damaris. "There's another one coming to join them."

"That's the boar," said Rory, "and that's exactly what he is."

"How d'you mean?"

"Haven't you ever heard him? Wordy, pompous, opinionated, thinks he's always right about everything, never listens to anyone else. The sows are bad enough, but he's the biggest bore of the lot. Listen to him now – grunt, grunt, grunt, snort, snort – what rubbish he's talking."

In fact, the boar was indulging in his

usual reply to his wives' usual greeting. The registered name on his pedigree was Firingclose General Lord Nicholas of Winningshot, but the sows simply called him General.

"Good morning, General," they all said as he came squelching up through the churned-up paddock. Then, with an inward sigh, each one of them tried hard to put her mind into neutral, knowing only too well what was coming.

"Ah, ladies," said the General in his deep voice. "Once again I find that I must question your customary greeting. There is no doubt that it is morning, but what precisely do you mean by 'good'? Virtuous? Pious? Kind? Well behaved? Worthy?"

"Sure and it isn't raining, General," said Mrs O'Bese.

"But," said the General, "is the absence of rainfall in itself good? Observe, for example, yonder duck, which to my surprise is consorting with a dog, an unlikely partnership in my opinion, of mammal and bird, of predator and prey, of . . . what was I saying?"

"Yonder duck," said Mrs Stout.

"Ah yes," said the General, "I recall. We were discussing the word 'good'. Such a beautiful morning as this may be good for us pigs, but I think, ladies, that we all know what kind of weather best pleases ducks.''

"Rain," said Mrs Portly, Mrs Chubby, Mrs Tubby, Mrs Swagbelly and Mrs Roly-Poly in tones of deepest boredom.

"Exactly," said the General.

He moved ponderously towards the orchard fence.

"Now then," he said, "I hope that all you ladies realize, thanks to my brief explanation, that what is a 'good' morning for a pig may not be a 'good' morning for a duck. Have I made myself clear?''

There was no reply, and the boar turned round to see that the seven sows had made themselves scarce.

"See what I mean?" said Rory. "He's bored 'em all to tears."

"Oh Rory!" Damaris cried. "He's

worse than the sows! I don't know how
they can stand him."

"I don't know how we stand the lot of
them," said Rory. "Not all farmers keep
pigs, you know, Mum told me. We're
just unlucky."

Damaris was silent for a while,
thinking.

34

Then she said, "You spoke of 'keeping' pigs. Well, that means managing them, looking after them, feeding them and so forth, I know that. But it also means keeping them *in*, doesn't it? There's pig-netting all round their paddock. But down the other end, near the road, there's a gate."

Rory sat up abruptly.

"You mean . . . ?" he said.

"I mean," said Damaris, "that if somehow or other that gate was to be opened, then those patronizing sows and that pontificating boar might just . . . what's the word I'm looking for?"

". . . emigrate!" cried Rory. "Damaris, you're a genius! Let's go and have a look at that gate right now. Race you!" and away he ran.

Damaris flew direct across the muddy pig paddock, but so speedy was the

sheepdog that they arrived at the gate at
much the same time. Rory stood on his
hindlegs to examine its fastening. Then
he dropped back down with a growl of
disappointment.

"Hopeless!" he said. "There's a special
sort of bolt we could never pull back, and
worse, it's padlocked."

Damaris ducked under the metal gate, whose bars were too close together to admit more than a pig's snout. She splattered about in the mud, testing it with her bill.

"We don't need to open the gate," she said.

"Oh, look," said Rory, "ducks may fly, but pigs can't. How are they going to get over it?"

"Under it," Damaris said.

"They're far too big."

"Not if a hole was dug under the gate," said Damaris. "A great big hole. In this nice soft earth. By you."

4. Pigs Stopped Play

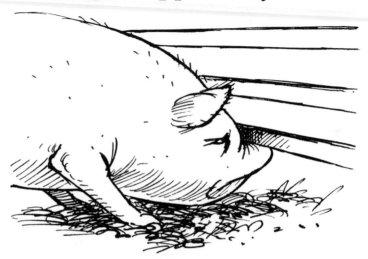

Very early the following morning, Rory did indeed dig that hole. Then he woke the pigs and said to the boar, very respectfully, "Would you be good enough to follow me, sir?"

At the gate he said, "Be kind enough to put your head under here, sir, and give a heave."

And, as the sows watched, the General put his great head in the hole and gave an almighty heave. Up came the gate, right off its hinges at one end, while at the other end, the bolt bent and the padlock snapped. Then down crashed the whole thing and away down the road went the sows, marching behind their master.

Before long there were grumblings of discontent in the ranks.

"I'm tired" and "My feet hurt" and "I'm starving hungry" and "I've had about enough of this", the sows complained, and finally the fattest of them, Mrs Roly-Poly, simply lay down in the road. Firingclose General Lord Nicholas of Winningshot heard the patter of hoofs cease behind him, and turned to see that all the sows had stopped.

"What is this?" he grunted. "Is this mutiny?"

"Don't know what the place is called, General," said Mrs Chubby, "but we're not going any further, not till we've had a rest and a bite to eat. My trotters is fair wore out."

This brought from the General a long lecture, very military in tone, on duty and discipline, and for a while the sows lay in the road, not listening to a word, but simply resting and getting their breath. But when the boar paused to get his, Mrs Tubby said, "Don't forget, General, that an army marches on its stomach."

The General glowered at her. Then it occurred to him that his own stomach was feeling remarkably empty.

"Mrs Tubby," he said, "you took the words right out of my mouth. I was merely waiting until we found a suitable source of food," and, after a short lecture on the importance of a balanced diet, he set off again, the sows reluctantly following.

Not half a mile on, they came upon an open gateway and, beyond it, a fine crop of sugar-beet.

Eagerly the hungry pigs fell upon this bonanza, tearing and swallowing the green leafy tops and ripping great chunks out of the sweet roots in the ground beneath, eating and eating until at last they could hold no more, and even the General was speechless.

They lay in the ruined crop and

snored, and none of them saw a brown-and-white duck flying over the sugar-beet field.

"Looks like they've struck it lucky," Damaris told Rory when she arrived back at the farm. "Took me a bit of time, but when I did find them, they'd gorged themselves in a field of roots and were all lying there, blown out like balloons."

"Good," said Rory. "The happier they are, the less they'll want to come back here. We don't want things to go wrong for them so that they start to wish they were safely back in their old paddock."

But it was not long before things started to go very wrong indeed for the General and his wives.

At first it looked as though he had led them to the promised land, so well did they feed. For a day and a half they stuffed themselves with sugar-beet and sugar-beet tops. There was even a pond in the corner of the field, where they could drink and wallow. But then they began to pay the price.

"I don't know why, dear," said Mrs Portly to Mrs Stout, "but my guts don't half feel funny."

"Mine too," said Mrs Stout, and the other sows grunted agreement.

Mrs O'Bese did not mince her words.

"I've got the trots," she said, and before long they all had, the General included.

"In my opinion," he said uncomfortably, "this unfortunate condition has been caused by an imprudent consumption of the fresh green tops of the sugar-beet, acting as a purgative."

"Tops or bottoms," said Mrs O'Bese, "I know which end of me is worse off.

Come on, General, let's be getting out of here."

So they did, marching off once more down the road and leaving upon its surface plentiful evidence of their troubles.

But worse was to come.

That afternoon the pigs reached the outskirts of a village. So far their journey had been through a countryside of few houses and isolated farms, but now they came upon a signpost, saying

MUDDLEHAMPTON ½

and shortly after that there was another open gateway with a notice-board fixed upon it that read

MUDDLEHAMPTON CRICKET CLUB
PRIVATE
TRESPASSERS WILL BE
PROSECUTED

But just how prosecuted they were about to be, the General and his followers were yet to realize.

Beset by their troubled stomachs, the sows turned in at the gateway. Beyond, they could see, was a large and well-mown field with, at its far end, a single-storeyed wooden building before which a lot of people were sitting in deck-chairs.

In the middle of the field was a number of other people all dressed in white.

As the pigs drew nearer, they could see one of these white-clad people appear to throw an object at another, who struck at it with a kind of wooden cudgel. The spectators began to clap, and there were cries of "Good shot!" and "Well hit!", while the umpire at the bowler's end prepared to signal what looked like a certain four. But before the

ball could reach the boundary, it reached
the General, who fielded it neatly in his
great jaws and started thoughtfully to
chew it. Meanwhile, the sows began to
root about in the well-kept grass,
ploughing their way purposefully
towards the pitch, while the shocked
players stood as though turned to stone.

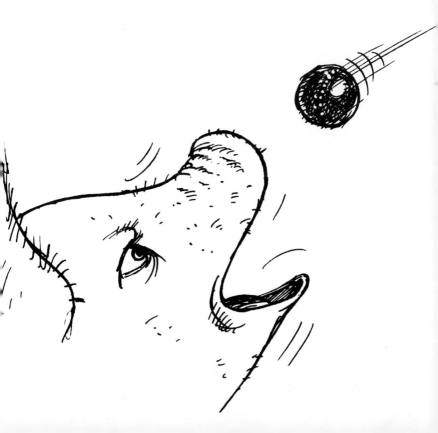

All eyes were on the pigs. No one noticed a brown-and-white duck circling overhead.

Then pandemonium broke loose as both the Muddlehampton First xi, who were fielding, and the two visiting batsmen sprang into action. The visitors led the charge, brandishing their bats, while with them ran six of the fielders, each waving a hastily uprooted stump, while the rest of the cricketers, plus the two umpires, rushed to join the fray.

The General and his wives galloped wildly about, squealing their dismay and leaving behind them in their fright much evidence of their recent unwise feasting.

Smack! went the bats on fat bottoms, Crack! went the stumps on broad backs, while several of the pursuing cricketers slipped and fell, adding a quite new colour to their snowy flannels. Until at last the invaders were driven out, and the match abandoned.

Muddlehampton's scorer was a stickler for the truth, and solemnly he wrote in his scorebook

PIGS STOPPED PLAY.

5. Mr Crook

After the scene on the cricket ground, Damaris had not returned to the farm. She was a fair-minded bird and, annoying though she had thought the pigs in the past, she began to feel sorry for them as they hurried off, now sore outside as well as inside. I must keep an eye on them for as long as I can, she thought. Perhaps someone else will give them a home.

And, shortly, someone else did.

Among the spectators at the cricket match had been a local livestock dealer called Crook, a name, some said, that suited him well, for some of his deals were a trifle shady.

As the General and his wives retreated, squealing, before the onslaught of bat and stump, Mr Crook wasted no time, but slipped behind the pavilion and out of the ground, making his hasty way across the fields to his yard a little distance beyond the village. Thus it was that the angry sows (for by now each blamed the General for her bellyaches and her bruises) and their defeated leader heard a familiar and most welcome sound.

"Pig! Pig! Pig! Pig!" crooned Mr Crook, appearing in the lane before them, rattling a bucket, and the General and his wives eagerly followed. In through a gate

they went, across a yard, and into a
loose-box.

As Mr Crook closed the lower part of
the stout door behind them and bolted it,
he heard a quacking, and, looking up,
saw a brown-and-white duck flying
around.

He thought nothing of it, for he was
too busy reckoning in his head what a
Large White boar and seven sows,

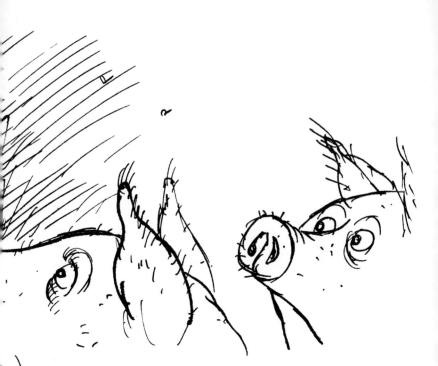

probably all in-pig, might fetch. He
leaned on the half-door and addressed
them.

"You lot can stop here," he said, "till
the fuss has died down, and if your
owner should come looking, I'll just say I
was keeping you safe for him. Then,
after a while, I'll take you to market, not
the local one, but a good way away.
Easiest money I've made in a long time.

Now then, it looks to me as if you've been eating summat you shouldn't. Starvation's the best cure for that sort of trouble, so no grub for you lot for a bit," and off he went.

Once he was out of sight, Damaris flew down to the loose-box. It isn't easy for ducks to perch like chickens, but the top of the half-door was quite wide, and she managed to balance upon it. Inside, there was a babble of noise, and it was plain to Damaris, listening, that the General was no longer in command.

"Now look what you've got us into," said one sow.

"First you walk the legs off us!"

"Then you let us eat all those sugar-beet tops!"

"And we get the trots!"

"Then we get beaten black and blue with clubs and sticks!"

"And finish up in this poky little hole!"

"With nothing to eat!"

"Ladies! Ladies! Please!" snorted the boar, but they took no notice of him.

"Calls himself a general," someone said. "A general disaster, he is!"

Not until the rumpus had died down did the sows notice Damaris perching on the half-door.

"Begorrah," said Mrs O'Bese, "isn't that the duck that knew the meaning of 'ignoramus'? She's a clever duck, that one is."

"Thank you," said Damaris.

She rather liked Mrs O'Bese, she suddenly realized, partly because of what she had just said, and partly because of the Irishness of her. Her heart, Damaris felt, was warmer than those of the others.

"Isn't it the lucky duck you are," went on Mrs O'Bese. "You can just fly home tonight. I wish I could. I wish we were all back home, well fed and housed in our old paddock, free to roam around and root about in the fresh air, instead of being stuck in this prison."

And a secure prison it looked to be. The floor was of concrete, and the strong wooden door, which opened inward, was faced with a large sheet of tin. No pig would ever be able to force it open.

"I'm beginning to feel sorry for them," Damaris said to Rory next morning, when she had told him all that had happened.

"I don't care about the pigs," said Rory, "but I'm beginning to feel sorry for the farmer. He's worried stiff, you can see it, driving about all over the place, every minute he can spare, looking for them."

"What are we to do?" said Damaris.

"We're going to have to tell the farmer where they are."

"Oh yes, and just how do we do that?"

Just then there came a shrill whistle.

"Here we go," said Rory. "You think of something, Damaris. If anyone can, you can."

Luvaduck, thought Damaris, I'm not *that* clever.

The farmer and his wife were sitting at breakfast the next morning.

"Where are you going to look today then, Jim?" asked the farmer's wife.

"Don't really know, Emma," said the farmer. "I've been everywhere – Muddlehampton, Muddlebury, Muddlechester, Upper Muddle, Lower Muddle."

At that moment they heard a tapping noise, and there, sitting on the window-sill outside and banging on the pane with her bill, was a brown-and-white duck.

"Whatever's she doing that for, silly

thing?" said the farmer's wife.

"Oh, that's Rory's pal, that is. Thick as thieves, they are. Never known a dog chum up with a duck before. You'd have thought Rory would have had more sense," said the farmer, and he rose and threw up the sash-window.

"What do you want, stupid?" he said.

For answer, Damaris let out a volley of excited quacks and flew away in the direction of Muddlehampton, calling loudly all the time.

"Perhaps she's trying to tell you something, Jim," said the farmer's wife.

"Oh, come on, Emma!" he replied. "Next thing you'll be saying she knows where the pigs are," and he shut the window.

Looking back, Damaris could see that no notice had been taken of her signals.

That afternoon Damaris flew all the way back to Mr Crook's yard and landed once again on top of the half-door of the loose-box. The pigs, she saw, now had a thick bed of straw, so that at least they looked a good deal cleaner.

"Hallo," she said. "How are things?"

"Terrible!" said a chorus of voices. "There's no room to move in here."

"Not even to swing the proverbial cat," said the General. "I fear that some of us are . . . what shall I say . . . getting upon each other's nerves."

"You're getting on everyone's nerves!" the sows shouted at him.

"See here, clever duck," said Mrs O'Bese. "Can you not help us?"

"I've tried," Damaris said, "but I can't think of a way."

"You wouldn't," said Mrs Stout. "You're not intelligent enough."

"Quite right, dear," said Mrs Portly.

Just then Damaris heard the noise of a door shutting on the other side of the yard.

There Mr Crook used a shed as his office, and, looking through its window, he saw a duck perched on the half-door of the loose-box. Mr Crook was very fond of ducks (with apple sauce and garden peas and new potatoes), and now he came out into the yard with his shotgun.

Damaris turned her head to see the man carrying what looked like a thick stick under his arm, and she took off and flew hurriedly up. Hardly had she aimed herself in the direction of home than she heard a tremendous bang and felt, all at the same time, the blast of the charge of shot as it whistled by her and a sudden agonizing pain in one wing.

6. The *Pig Breeders' Gazette*

There had been only one thought in Damaris's head and that had been of flight, to get away, as quickly and as far as possible, from the menace of the man with the gun. But flight was now beyond her powers.

Unbalanced, beating wildly but fruitlessly with her one good wing, Damaris tumbled out of the sky.

Yet she was destined to be lucky.

Through the valley in which all the

villages lay ran the River Muddle, and into it, mercifully, Damaris now fell with a great splash. Though she could no longer fly, she could swim, and she paddled hastily away.

So that by the time Mr Crook reached the river bank, intending to finish off his wounded prey, Damaris was nowhere to be seen.

Again by luck, the farm lay

downstream from Muddlehampton so
that she was swimming with the current.
But after some time her homing instincts
told her that soon she would be carried
too far. I can't fly, she said to herself,
and there's no point in swimming any
further or I shall end up in the sea, so I
must get out and walk.

Normally she would have made for
home the shortest way – as the crow, or,

in this case, the duck, flies. But that
would have meant tramping across
country through hedges and over fences
and standing crops, so she went as a
human would have done, by road. And
still, as if to make up for misfortune, her
luck held. Ducks are some of the world's
worst walkers, and after almost a mile of
waddling, Damaris was tiring rapidly,

her injured wing throbbing, her legs aching, her head beginning to spin, when she heard the sound of an approaching motor.

There, coming towards her, was the farmer's pick-up truck.

As it reached her, it stopped and Rory leaped down from the back and ran to her.

"What's the matter?" he said.

"I've been shot," said Damaris.

"What's the matter, Rory?" called his mother Tess.

"She's been shot," said Rory.

"What's the matter, duck?" said the farmer, getting down from his cab.

"I've been shot," quacked Damaris, and "She's been shot" barked the two sheepdogs, but, of course, he did not understand. She was hurt though – he could see that – and the farmer carefully picked her up and put her on the passenger seat and turned for home.

"I reckon this bird's been shot, Emma," he said to his wife as he brought the duck into the kitchen. "It's a funny thing, but about an hour ago Rory here came into the milking-parlour whining and whimpering as though he was worried stiff about something."

"He knew his friend was in trouble, you mean, Jim?"

"Could be. Animals know things we couldn't know. Hold her a minute while I have a look at this wing."

Gently he stretched it.

"Don't think anything's broken," he said. "Ah, look, I see. I was right, someone's had a bang at her. There's a little cluster of shot right in the angle of the wing joint, can you see, little black things just under the skin."

He looked at his watch.

"The vet won't have finished his evening surgery yet," he said. "Come on, duck, off we go again."

The vet had extracted all the pellets, and then bandaged Damaris right round the middle, pinning both wings to her sides. Still woozy from the anaesthetic, she spent that night in a large cardboard box beside the Aga.

"We don't want her flapping about, not for a day or two," the vet had said. "Give things time to heal. She's been lucky."

By morning Damaris felt a different duck. Her injured wing was stiff and sore certainly, but she was safe and at home and well looked after. The farmer and his wife fed her and fussed over her, and even Tess bothered to look into the box and say "Better?"

As for Rory, his concern for his friend was so obvious that the farmer decided to excuse him from duty.

The farmer's wife came and lifted Damaris out of the cardboard box: she had lined it with newspapers that were by now extremely messy, and she replaced them with a fresh layer.

It so happened that one of these was a

Large White Championship

magazine, an old copy of the *Pig Breeders' Gazette*, and when Damaris was replaced in the box, she noticed what she was about to sit on.

The print, of course, meant nothing to her – "Large White boar wins Supreme Championship at the Royal Show" was to her a lot of little black squiggles – but the picture below immediately caught her eye.

It was the spitting image of the General.

Something clicked in Damaris's unusually large brain.

Here was a way to communicate with the farmer!

Not by word of mouth – she couldn't speak to him.

Not by her actions – she had tried flying away and calling to him to follow, but in vain.

But how about a pictorial message? Show him the picture!

"Rory," she said, "look in here."

Rory peered into the box.

"It's a picture of a pig," he said.

"Yes. Can you get it out?"

Damaris stood to one side as the sheepdog put his head into the box and carefully picked up the magazine in his mouth.

"Put it on the floor, pig upwards," she said.

He did.

"Now, do you see what I'm getting at?"

"No."

"Listen then."

Rory listened as Damaris explained her idea.

Then he said, "Brilliant! But are they clever enough to get the message?"

"You've got it," said Damaris, "and
they're meant to be more intelligent than
any dog."

"Or even any pig."

"And certainly any duck."

"Except one," said Rory proudly.

The farmer's wife came into the
kitchen.

"Go on, Rory," quacked Damaris
softly.

Rory began to bark excitedly. He bounced about beside the *Pig Breeders' Gazette*, putting a paw on the picture, scratching at it, pointing his muzzle at it, doing everything in his power to get the woman to look at it.

She did.

"Whatever's the matter, Rory?" she said.

The farmer came in.

"Whatever's the matter with Rory?" he said.

"He's trying to tell us something."

At that moment Damaris joined in. She could not flap her wings because of the bandaging, but she quacked as loudly as she could. The farmer's wife lifted her out of the cardboard box and put her down on the floor beside the magazine, and Damaris began to tap with her bill upon the picture of the Supreme

74

Champion Large White.

"She's trying to tell us something, too," she said. "About our pigs, it must be."

"There you go again, Emma," the farmer said. "Trying to tell me that these two know where the pigs are."

"Remember what you said, Jim. 'Animals know things we couldn't know.' Those were your very words."

"Yes, but I was talking about a dog like Rory. There's no such thing as a clever duck, not outside of a children's story book."

7. Market Day

"Anyway," said the farmer, "I'd best be off on my usual search. I must have looked in almost every field in this valley. Someone must have them shut up somewhere."

"You're just taking Tess?" his wife said.

"Yes."

But as he went out of the kitchen, Rory followed and at his heels Damaris came waddling as fast as she could.

The farmer's wife went to the front door to see them off. The dogs had as usual jumped up into the bed of the truck. Damaris was standing waiting by the passenger door.

"You'll have to take her, Jim," the farmer's wife said.

"She won't be able to see anything, she's too short."

"You'll just have to stop every so often and lift her out and let her have a look round. If she quacks and Rory barks, like they've just been doing, I reckon you're getting warm. Try all the villages in turn."

Some time after the pick-up truck had gone off down the farm road, a cattle lorry drove into Mr Crook's yard. It was market day in a distant town, and the dealer reckoned he had waited long enough. Whoever owns these pigs, he said to himself, must have given up hope by now.

Meanwhile the farmer had driven in turn to the villages of Muddlebury, Muddlechester, Upper Muddle and Lower Muddle. Near each he had stopped and, feeling a fool, had lifted Damaris out. But she had made no sound. Each time, Rory had barked, but Damaris remained silent.

The dog barks at the smell of pigs, any pigs, the farmer thought, but will the duck only quack at the right pigs? What am I saying? The duck knows more than the dog? I'm beginning to believe it.

In a lane outside Muddlehampton, not far from the River Muddle, he stopped and lifted Damaris out once more.

Immediately she began to quack loudly and to struggle wildly in his arms. Hearing her, Rory let out a volley of barks and Tess, of course, joined in.

"What's all that racket, boss?" said the haulier to Mr Crook as they raised the tail-board behind the pigs and clamped it shut, and at that moment they saw a pick-up truck come to a stop in the yard gateway, blocking it.

From it jumped a man holding in his arms a bandaged duck and followed by two sheepdogs. The dogs were barking and growling, the duck was quacking madly, and the man, who looked angry, walked up to Mr Crook and said, "What have you got in that lorry?"

"Mind your own business," said the dealer.

"It *is* my business," said the farmer.

"You've got a pedigree Large White boar and seven sows in there, haven't you?"

The haulier's jaw dropped.

"Here," he said, "how did you know that?"

"There's something else I know too," said the farmer.

He took a notebook out of his pocket.

"Now then," he said to the dealer, "here are all the numbers on the ear-tags

of these pigs. Let's have a look and see if they match, shall we?"

Mr Crook knew when he was beaten.

"Hang on a bit," he said to his haulier, and he took the farmer across the yard to his office.

"Am I pleased to see you, sir!" he said. "I've been keeping those pigs safe, hoping someone would claim them. Couldn't afford to keep them any longer, you know – eating me out of house and home. Just loading them up to send to a friend of mine that's got a bit of rough ground . . ."

"Don't bother spinning me a cock-and-bull story about it," said the farmer. "I know the dates of the markets. I'll tell you where you're sending them and that's straight to my farm. You'll pay the haulage of course."

"They've cost me a lot already," said Mr Crook sullenly.

"And they'd have earned you a nice lot too if I hadn't turned up," said the farmer.

"How did you know where to come?"

The farmer looked at the dealer.

Then he looked at Damaris.

Then he looked at a shotgun, propped in the corner of the office.

Then he suddenly knew, beyond a shadow of a doubt, what had happened.

"The duck told me," he said. "I'll send you the vet's bill."

Mr Crook mopped his face with a large spotted handkerchief. "No need for us to say anything to anybody else about all this business, is there, sir?" he said.

"No need at all," said the farmer. "And I'll tell the duck to keep quiet about it too."

8. Clever Duck!

"There's no place like home," grunted
Mrs Stout to Mrs Portly as the pigs made
their way down the tail-board of the
cattle lorry and through the freshly
mended gate into their old paddock.

"Quite right, dear," said Mrs Portly.

"Journey's end," said Mrs O'Bese,
"and it was a miserable old journey, so it
was."

"Hear, hear!" said Mrs Chubby, Mrs
Tubby, Mrs Swagbelly and Mrs Roly-Poly.

Only Firingclose General Lord Nicholas of Winningshot said nothing. The promised land had not lived up to its promise, and for once he thought it wise to keep his mouth shut. What's more, he soon found that he no longer had one of the two pig huts to himself, for the sows took over both of them, and grumbled loudly when he meekly tried to push in, so that he often found himself sleeping outside. A male chauvinist pig he may once have been, but now he was to his wives just a boring old boar and they did not hesitate to tell him so.

Two months later, however, the General had the paddock to himself. His wives had all been moved to a range of farrowing houses to await the birth of their children.

Damaris felt sorry for the boar. Once her wing was fully healed, she flew over now and again for a chat. Not that she got a word in edgewise. The General had lost much of his authority, but none of his gift of the gab. He appeared quite unaware of the duck's part in the rescue, as indeed were all the sows except one.

Maybe it had something to do with Mrs O'Bese's Celtic blood, but she alone mentioned it when Damaris went visiting the expectant mothers.

"Sure and it was you that found us, wasn't it, duck?" she said. "I knew you were the clever one, right from the start. 'If you don't know what an ignoramus is,' you said, 'then you must be one.' Begorrah, you could have knocked me down with a duck's feather. And I never thought much of ducks before."

"Why not?" said Damaris.

"Too stupid, I thought. Don't know anything."

"Actually," said Damaris, "I never thought much of pigs before."

"Why not?" said Mrs O'Bese.

"Too clever by half. Think they know everything."

Mrs O'Bese gave a fusillade of little grunts that sounded like "Ha! Ha! Ha! Ha!"

"I know one thing, duck," she said. "I like you, so I do. Good luck to you."

"Thanks," said Damaris, "and I hope all your troubles will be little ones."

Which they were, because before long all the sows farrowed.

Most had eight, nine or ten piglets, but Mrs O'Bese, just to be different, gave birth to no less than thirteen little half-Irish babies.

"Let us only hope," she said, "that they don't grow up to be as long-winded as their dada, or it will be an unlucky number."

"I like that Irish sow," said Damaris to Rory. They were having one of their evening conversations out in the orchard, Rory lying in the grass, Damaris squatting beside him.

"She's the best of a bad lot," said Rory, "but none of them has changed really. They still patronize all the other animals on the farm. They still think they're the greatest and they don't hide the fact."

"Look at those two, Emma," said the farmer to his wife, as side by side they leaned against the orchard gate, enjoying the end of the day.

"It's the strangest friendship, Jim," she said.

"That's the strangest duck," he said. "I've said it many times before, I know, but she saved us a packet of money. We'd never have seen our pigs again, and that dealer would have been laughing. She found them, all by herself."

"And could have lost her life."

"Yes. Why should a duck worry about pigs? She goes visiting them, you know. I saw her today, quacking away to that

old Irish sow and the sow grunting back
at her. Look at her now, bending Rory's
ear about something or other. I'd dearly
love to understand what animals say to
one another."

"Look at the farmer and his wife
chatting away, Rory," Damaris said. "I'd
dearly love to understand what humans
say to one another."

"That," said Rory, "is one thing you're never going to be able to do. I can understand the odd word – 'Come by!', 'Away to me!', 'Down', 'Stay' – that sort of thing. But most of what they say is gibberish."

He got up and moved towards the two people, Damaris waddling behind.

"Listen," he said. "They'll say

something when we reach them," and when they did, the man patted him and said a couple of words.

"I got that," Rory said. "He's telling me I'm a good dog."

The woman bent down and stroked Damaris's brown-and-white plumage, and she too spoke two words.

"What did she say to me?" asked Damaris.

"Haven't a clue," replied Rory, as the farmer's wife said once more "Clever duck!"